Barbie™
Enchanted Fairy Tales

Retold by Jill L. Goldowsky

Photography by Scott Fujikawa, Laura Lynch, Susan Cracraft,
Tim Geisen, Mark Adams, Lisa Collins, and Judy Tsuno

Contents

Reader's Digest
Children's Books™

Pleasantville, New York • Montréal, Québec • Bath, United Kingdom

Snow White and the Seven Dwarfs

Once upon a time, a king and queen had a baby girl of extraordinary beauty, with hair as dark as night, lips as red as roses, and skin as white as snow. She was so pretty that her mother gave her the name Snow White. She was as good-natured a child as she was beautiful.

When Snow White's mother passed away, the king married another woman. His new queen was beautiful, too, but she thought only of her own looks and did not like it one bit that Snow White was so lovely. One day, she thought, Snow White could become even more beautiful than herself! For reassurance, the queen would look at her reflection in her magic mirror and ask:

Mirror, mirror on the wall,
Who is fairest of us all?
And the mirror would always reply:
You, queen, are the fairest of all.
The queen was very happy to hear these words because she knew that her magic mirror always told her the truth. But Snow White continued to grow more beautiful with every passing day. Finally, the mirror answered:
You are fair, my queen, it is true.
But Snow White is far fairer than you.
When the queen heard these words, she was filled with rage. She hated Snow White for being more beautiful and wanted her dead. Immediately, she called for her huntsman and ordered him to kill her.

"Take Snow White far into the forest so that I may never see her again," she said. "And bring me back her heart so that I know for sure that she is dead."

4

The huntsman feared for his own life if he did not obey the queen's orders, so he took Snow White deep in the forest. Snow White begged him to let her go. "I promise to wander off into the deepest part of the wood. I'll never return home again if you would just spare me my life."

The huntsman liked Snow White and didn't want to kill her. So he left her behind in the forest and brought the queen the heart of a wild beast instead.

Snow White was scared in the forest all by herself. Unusual shadows and strange noises frightened her. Finally, she could stand it no longer. She ran as far and fast as her legs would take her. At last, she came to a little cottage and decided to go inside to rest.

Who lives in such a little house? she wondered, as she ducked through the door. She noticed that everything inside was small and neat, and after her dreadful day in the forest, she found the

place very comforting. Seven chairs were set around a table, each with its own place setting, and seven little cots were lined up neatly all in a row. She ate a piece of bread from the table and then went to rest on a cozy little bed.

Later that evening, seven dwarfs returned home to their cottage after working a long day in the mines. And to their surprise, there they found a beautiful girl lying fast asleep!

"Goodness gracious!" they exclaimed. "What a lovely child she is."

The seven dwarfs were curious to learn who the strange girl was, but she looked too peaceful to be disturbed. When she awoke the next morning and saw the seven little men watching her, she was frightened, but they quickly made her feel at ease. They were so friendly and kind that she liked them right away.

"I am Snow White," she said.

"Why did you come to our house?" the dwarfs wanted to know.

And then Snow White told her new friends how her stepmother wanted her dead, how the huntsman let her go, and how she ran through the forest terrified, until she saw their cottage. The seven

dwarfs felt sorry for Snow White and asked her to stay with them.

Snow White lived very happily with the dwarfs. Together they would sing and dance, and while the dwarfs were at work, Snow White kept house for them. Every day before the dwarfs left for the mines,

they told her not to answer the door for anyone. They didn't want the evil queen to find her there.

Back at the castle, the queen went to her magic mirror and asked:

Mirror, mirror on the wall
Who is fairest of us all?

And the mirror replied:

You are fair, my queen, it is true.
But Snow White is far fairer than you.

"Snow White must still be alive!" shouted the queen, furiously. And right at that moment she came up with a plan to kill the beautiful girl herself.

The next day, Snow White was sweeping the cottage floor when she heard a knock at the door. She peaked out of the tiny window to see who it was and saw a poor old lady with a basket of red apples. The apples looked so delicious that Snow White could think of nothing else.

Surely an old lady with apples like these could do me no harm, thought Snow White. *I'm certain the dwarfs would not mind if I let her in.* So she opened the door and eagerly bit into the juicy, red apple that the lady offered her.

Of course, the old woman was really Snow White's wicked stepmother in disguise, and the delicious-looking apples she had with her were poisonous. As soon as Snow White took a bite, she fell to the floor as though she was dead.

The queen was very pleased to see Snow White stumble to the ground. She was happy to be rid of her rival at last. When she arrived back at the castle she went straight to her magic mirror and asked:

Mirror, mirror on the wall,
Who is fairest of us all?

And the mirror replied,
You, queen, are the fairest of all.

That night, the seven dwarfs returned home to find their precious Snow White lying still on the floor.

"Oh, no!" they cried. "What has become of Snow White?"

The seven little men tried everything they could to make Snow White come back to life, but nothing worked. She lay still, looking as lovely as ever.

The dwarfs cried for days and then finally decided to put Snow White in a glass case and bring her to the top of a hill where they would watch over her. She was still beautiful—hair as dark as night, lips as red as roses, and skin as white as snow—and they wanted her beauty to be seen by all who passed.

Then one day, a prince was riding on his horse over the hill and he saw the beautiful princess inside the glass case. As soon as he laid eyes on her, he knew that he could not live without her. He told this to the dwarfs who guarded her body and they allowed him to open the glass case to kiss her. Just then, as he lifted Snow White in his arms the poisonous piece of apple inside her mouth fell out and her eyes fluttered open. The evil queen's spell was undone! To Snow White's surprise, she awoke in the arms of a prince, and she fell in love with him at first sight.

The prince asked Snow White to marry him and Snow White could not have been happier. Filled with joy, the dwarfs danced around them—prince and princess.

As for the queen, when she found out about Snow White she grew miserable and jealous. In the end, all the hatred she felt for Snow White made her so ugly that even the magic mirror didn't want to look at her. At last, she lost all her magic powers, and she was never able to harm the beautiful Snow White—or her prince—ever again.

Hansel and Gretel

Long ago, there lived a woodcutter and his family along the edge of a big forest. He had a wife and two children, Hansel and Gretel, and they were very poor. The children were fond of their father, but not their stepmother, who treated them badly. At last there came a day when they were so poor that there simply was not enough food for them all. Hansel and Gretel heard their father talking to their stepmother.

"What is to become of us?" he asked. "There is so little food that we may all starve to death."

"I have a plan," said his wife. "Tomorrow we will take the children deep into the forest and pretend to search for wood. Then we will leave them there and they won't be able to find their way back home."

The woodcutter did not want to abandon his children. He loved them dearly. But his selfish wife convinced him that it would be better to leave the children in the forest than for all of them to die at home.

After hearing these words, Gretel wept softly. But Hansel was brave and said, "Do not worry, Gretel. I will find a way to save us."

The next morning, the woodcutter's wife woke the two children like she planned. "Get up, you lazy things," she said. "We're going into the forest to gather wood." She gave them each a small crust of dry bread and said, "This is all the food there is, so don't waste it." Obediently, Hansel and Gretel put their crusts of bread into their pockets and saved them for later.

The woodcutter and his wife led the two children into the forest. They walked for a long time, and as they walked, the children lagged behind and Hansel secretly broke off little pieces from the bread inside his pocket. He planned to leave a trail of breadcrumbs for him and Gretel to follow back home.

When the woodcutter and his wife thought they were inside the forest deep enough to lose the children, they stopped and made a fire.

"You children stay here," said the stepmother. "We will return for you when your father and I finish chopping wood."

But Hansel and Gretel both knew the truth—they were not coming back. They tried to make Gretel's bread last, but by dark they were tired and very hungry. They finished the last of the bread and slept by the light of the fire until morning. When they awoke, they searched for the trail of bread Hansel had left, but mice had come during the night and eaten it all. Not a crumb was left to guide them back home.

"We will find a path out of the woods," Hansel stoutly assured his sister. But they wandered through the forest for a day and a night and could find no way out.

At last, the children were so exhausted that they stopped by a tree and fell asleep. Hours later they awoke to the sweet song of a beautiful bird. When it finished singing, it flapped its wings and flew on in front of them. It lead them straight to a little house made of candy!

Hansel and Gretel ran toward the house. "What a great feast we shall have!" exclaimed Hansel. He broke off pieces of the candy-cane posts while Gretel tasted the spun-sugar windows. Then from inside the house a voice called:

Nibble, nibble like a mouse,
Who is nibbling at my house?

Frightened, Hansel and Gretel dropped their food. A lady came to the door, "Oh, my dears!" she exclaimed. "You must be starving! Please stay—eat all you want." Then she invited them inside and made up comfortable beds for them to sleep in that night. Hansel and Gretel felt like they were in heaven.

What they didn't know was that the lady was really a wicked witch! She lured children inside with sweets from her delicious house, and then she fattened them up to make them into stew! And s[o] just before morning came, the witch sto[le] Hansel from his bed, and put him in a cage. "You are going to make a mighty fine dish," she cackled.

Then she woke Gretel and made her cook something for her brother to eat. The children cried and begged to be set free, but the witch just laughed at them

Every day, the witch checked Hansel to see if he was fat enough to make into a meal. She made him stick out his finger to check how plump he was. But Hansel knew that the witch didn't have very good eyesight so he gave her an old chicken bone to feel instead! Hansel did this for many weeks, and the witch grew impatient.

What is taking so long to fatten him up? she wondered. Finally, she decided that she couldn't wait any longer.

"Gretel! Go fetch some water to boil," she ordered. "Even if Hansel is thin, I am going to make him my supper!"

Poor Gretel. She cried for her brother. But the witch shouted at her to be quiet and demanded that she help her.

"Heat the oven," she ordered and pushed the girl forward. "Then stick your head inside and tell me if it is hot enough." The witch wanted to push Gretel into the oven and close the door so that she would cook, too.

But Gretel was smart. She knew what the witch was planning. "I do not know what you mean," she said innocently. "Please show me how to do it."

"You dumb girl!" screamed the witch as she poked her head in the oven. "You do it like this!"

And with a mighty push, Gretel shoved the witch all the way into the oven and shut the iron door. In an instant, the witch was gone forever.

Gretel ran to free Hansel from the cage and together they rejoiced that the witch was dead. Then they found boxes filled with gold and jewels in the witch's house. With nothing to fear, they happily filled their pockets with as many riches as possible before leaving the witch's prison.

As they searched for a way back home once more, Hansel and Gretel came to a big lake. *How shall we ever cross the water?* Hansel wondered. Suddenly, a white swan swam into view. Gretel asked if it would carry them to the other side.

The good swan was happy to help the children across the lake, and when they reached the other side, the forest began to look familiar to them.

"Look!" cried Hansel, after they had walked for a bit. "There's our cottage!" At once, Hansel and Gretel ran for the door. But the woodcutter had already seen them coming. He ran out to greet them and gave them great big hugs and kisses. His wife had disappeared, and he hadn't been happy since the day he left his children in the forest. He was filled with joy that they had found their way home.

Hansel and Gretel emptied their pockets and presented their father with all the treasures they had collected from the witch. The woodcutter was pleased with his children and very proud of their courage. From that day on, they were never to be hungry again. Hansel, Gretel, and their father lived happily, forever after.

Rumpelstiltzkin

Once upon a time, a poor miller and his beautiful daughter lived in a cottage near the king's castle. One day, the miller was walking near the palace at the same time the king was taking his leisurely stroll. The miller, who was very excited to meet his majesty, wanted the king to think that he was a person of great importance. So when he presented himself to the king, the miller bragged that his lovely daughter could spin straw into gold, even though she couldn't.

The king was a wealthy man and did not need any more gold, but he was interested in the girl's talent and said, "If your daughter is as clever as you say she is, bring her to my palace tomorrow morning."

When the miller's daughter arrived, the king brought her into a room filled with straw from top to bottom. He showed her the spinning wheel and said, "You have all day and all night to spin the straw into gold. And if you have not finished by morning, you shall die." Then he locked the girl inside the room, with only piles of straw, a stool, and the spinning wheel to keep her company.

The poor girl! She had no idea how to spin straw into gold! She sat down on the stool and wept for hours.

Suddenly, the door flew open and in walked a tiny man who was quite funny looking. "Good evening, pretty maiden," said the man. "Why are you so sad?"

"Oh!" sobbed the miller's daughter. "I must spin all this straw into gold for the king or I shall die, and I don't have a clue as to how to do it."

"Is that all?" said the man, as if it was a very simple thing to do. "I know how to spin straw into gold. What will you give me if I do it for you?"

"You may have my necklace," answered the miller's daughter graciously, as she unclasped it from her neck.

The little man accepted the necklace and sat down at the spinning wheel. Away it whirled, spinning the straw into gold. He worked and worked all through the night. By sunrise, the whole room of straw was transformed into spools of glittering gold. Then the man disappeared as suddenly as he had arrived.

The king opened the door as soon as the little man was gone and was delighted by what he saw. He was so impressed by the sight of

all the gold that it made him hungrier for more. He led the miller's daughter to an even bigger room, had it filled with even more straw, and told her to spin it into gold or she would die.

Once again the girl began to cry—she still had no idea how to spin straw into gold! And then suddenly, the door flew open again and in walked the strange man from the night before.

"What will you give me this time if I spin the straw into gold for you?" he asked.

"I will give you this ring," she said gratefully, as she slipped it off her finger.

The man accepted the ring and began to spin the straw into gold once more. The spinning wheel whirled as he worked and by morning the room was no longer filled with piles of straw, but with spools of glittering gold. Then he disappeared.

As soon as the sun rose, the king entered the room and was amazed once more by all the sparkling gold. He could not believe his eyes, but he was still not satisfied. *This is a talent worth keeping,* he thought. *She may just be a miller's daughter, but I will never find a richer girl.* So he led the miller's daughter to the largest room in the castle and filled it with straw until it was packed all the way to the ceiling!

"You must spin all this straw into gold by morning. If you do, I will make you my queen," he said. "If not, you shall die." Then he left the room and locked the door.

Still not knowing how to spin straw into gold, the miller's daughter again feared for her life. But she hoped that the little man would appear for a third time to help her. Sure enough, the door soon flew open and in walked the little man.

"What will you give me if I spin the straw into gold for you this time?" asked the man.

"I have nothing left to give," she said. "You have already taken everything I own."

"Then you must give me your first-born child when you are queen," he said.

The poor girl was so desperate for her life that she did not refuse. *Besides,* she thought, *I won't have a child for a long time, and by then the little man will have forgotten what he asked for.*

Once she agreed, the man immediately set out to work. He worked hard all night and spun each piece of straw into gold. When the king arrived the next morning and saw the roomful of gold, he was so pleased that he married the miller's daughter that very day.

The months passed quickly, and when one year had gone by, the queen gave birth to a beautiful baby. In that time, she had forgotten all about the strange man, but he didn't forget about her. When the baby was but a month

old, the little man appeared before her. "I have come to take your child," he said.

The queen was very upset by this and started to cry. She pleaded with him to take all the riches in the kingdom instead—anything, if she could just keep her baby. But the man would accept nothing other than the child.

The queen begged and cried so bitterly that the man at last felt sorry for her.

"I will give you three days and three nights to guess my name," he said. "And if you guess correctly, you may keep your child."

At once the queen began to call out all the different names she could think of. But after each name she mentioned, the man said, "No, that is not my name."

The next day the queen was ready with a lengthy list of the strangest and most uncommon names she could find. She even sent her messengers far and wide to find them.

"Are you Caspar? Melchior? Balthasar?" she asked.

"No," said the man.

"Are you Sheepshanks? Spindleshanks? Crookshanks?" she asked again.

"No," he said.

On the third day, one of the queen's messengers came to her with news. "I have no new names," he said. "But as I was walking through a forest, I came across a little man dancing around a campfire. This is what he sang:

Today I brew, tomorrow I bake,
And then the queen's dear child I'll take.
She does not know, that royal dame,
That Rumpelstiltzkin is my name!"

The queen prepared for the little man's visit with great relief. When he arrived, he was grinning from ear to ear, certain that the queen was not going to guess his name and that he'd have her child at last!

"Is your name Conrad?" asked the queen.

"No," replied the man with a smile.

"Is it Cuteska?" she asked.

"No," he said again.

"Well then, perhaps your name is Rumpelstiltzkin," she said sweetly.

The little man could not believe his ears! "How did you guess my name?" he shouted at the queen.

Then the man grew so angry that he stamped his foot so hard that it went right through the floor! Finally, the ground swallowed him up completely and he was gone. From that moment, Rumpelstiltzkin was never seen again, and the queen and her child lived happily ever after.

The Frog Prince

Long ago, there lived a king and his very beautiful daughter. Every day the princess would walk through her father's gardens to the palace well and sit at its edge to play with her favorite toy, a golden ball. The princess enjoyed tossing the ball into the air and then catching it in her hands. She played this game more than any other, and she never grew tired of it.

One day at the well, the princess threw the golden ball up toward the sky, and waited for it to fall back down into her hands. But this time the princess did not catch it. Instead—*kerplunk!*—it fell right into the well. The golden ball was gone.

"Oh, no!" cried the princess. "I will never play with my golden ball again!" Tears rolled down her cheeks as she mourned the loss of her plaything. She cried so hard that she almost didn't hear a small voice from behind.

"What is the matter, Princess?"

The princess turned around to see a fat, green frog with sad, bulging eyes.

"I'm crying over my golden ball," she said. "It has fallen into the well!"

"I can get your ball back for you," offered the frog. "But what will you give me in return?"

"Oh, anything you wish!" exclaimed the princess. "I promise to give you whatever you want. My dresses, my jewelry—even the sparkling crown I wear on my head."

"All those things sound very nice but I don't want them. I am very lonely, and want you to be my friend. Bring me to your home where I can sit beside you at the dinner table, eat from your plate, drink from your cup, sleep in your bed, and play with you during the day. If you promise me all these things, then I will go to the bottom of the well and bring you back your golden ball."

The princess wanted to have her ball back very badly, so she promised all of this to the frog—even though she had no intention of taking him home with her. She was repulsed by this green creature with bulging eyes and figured he couldn't live outside of the water, anyway.

True to his word, the frog dove down into the depths of the well as soon as the princess declared her promise, and returned with the golden ball. The princess was so happy to have her precious toy back that she quickly skipped off to the palace without even a word of thanks to the frog.

"Wait for me," the frog called from the well. "I can't hop that fast!"

But the princess did not care about the promise she made. She hurried back to the palace, and soon forgot about the ugly green frog.

The next day, as the princess was eating dinner with the king, she heard a tiny voice shout, "Daughter of the king, open the door. Remember the promise you made to me."

Who could that be? wondered the princess. She rose from the table to open the door, and by her feet stood a familiar

green creature. She slammed the door as quickly as she had opened it.

"What's wrong, my dear?" asked the king. "Who terrifies you so?"

"Oh, father!" cried the princess. "Yesterday I lost my golden ball in the well, and while I was crying, this horrid frog said he would get it back for me, but only if I promised to be his playmate."

"Did you make the promise to him?" asked the king.

"Yes," answered the princess, timidly.

"And did he give you back your ball?" pressed the king.

"Yes," the princess answered again.

"Then, my child, you must keep your promise. It is the only right thing to do. You should not make a promise if you do not intend to keep it."

The princess knew in her heart that her father was right. Reluctantly, she opened the door again and let the creature with the sad, bulging eyes inside.

"Lift me up beside you so I can eat from your plate and drink from your cup," demanded the frog.

The princess shuddered. She did not want to share her dinner with this creature! But there was no escaping it.

The king gave her a firm look that said, "You must keep your promise."

Before long, the frog was done with his meal and let out a croak of contentment. Then he asked the princess to carry him to her bedroom so he could fall asleep. The princess quivered at the thought of the slimy creature sleeping in her room. It was bad enough that he had to eat from her plate and drink from her cup—but to sleep in her bed, too? Again, her father gave her a stern look and she obeyed.

Once inside her bedroom, the princess dropped the frog into a corner on the floor and went to bed. But as she was drifting off to sleep, she heard a *thumpity thump*. Startled, she saw the frog hopping across the floor to her bed. "I would much rather sleep under your pillow," he said.

"You ask for too much," said the princess. "You may not sleep under my pillow."

"Then I will get the king," said the frog. "He will insist that you keep your promise." The princess knew the frog was right. So she picked him up and placed him under her pillow. Soon they were both fast asleep.

The next morning, the frog crawled out from beneath the princess's pillow and jumped off the bed. The princess opened

her eyes and saw the frog hopping back to the corner of her room.

Maybe it would be nice to have him for a friend, she thought. Feeling badly about the way she had treated him the day before, the princess wanted to apologize. She walked over to the frog, gently picked him up in her hand, and gave him a kiss. But just as her lips touched his green skin, something magical began to happen. All of a sudden, standing by her side, was a young and very handsome prince!

"Princess, I wasn't what I seemed to be," explained the prince. "I waited by the well for someone as special as you to help me undo a spell a wicked woman placed on me a long time ago. She turned me into a frog, but now you saved me because you kept your promise to be my friend."

The princess was very surprised to see such a handsome gentleman standing before her. "I haven't been a very good friend to you," she bowed her head in shame. "I hope you can find it in your heart to forgive me."

"You *have* been a good friend," replied the prince. "You were true to your word."

The prince and princess went to the well where they first met and played with the golden ball. In time, they became the best of friends and fell in love. At last, they were married, and at the ceremony, they promised to be each other's dear companions for the rest of their lives.

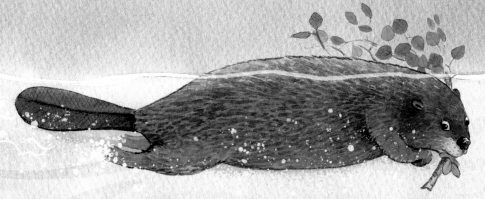

BEAVER
and OTTER
GET ALONG
...Sort of

A Story of Grit and Patience
between Neighbors

Words by Sneed B. Collard III

Pictures by Meg Sodano

To my daughter, Tessa, proud owner of
"Lola the otter dog." Love, Daddy.

—SC

For Byron and Leila who, despite their
differences, always got along.

—MS

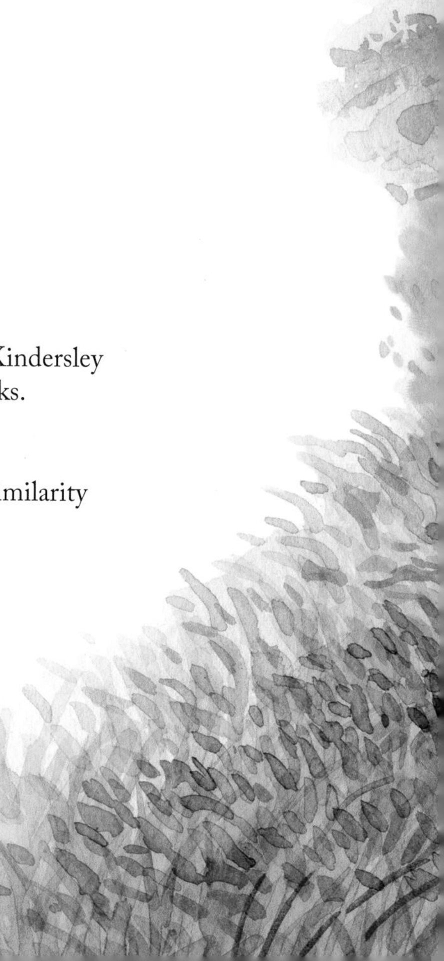

Published by Dawn Publications, an imprint of Sourcebooks eXplore
The characters and events portrayed in this book are fictitious or are used fictitiously. Any similarity
to real persons, living or dead, is purely coincidental and not intended by the author.
P.O. Box 4410, Naperville, Illinois 60567–4410
(630) 961-3900
sourcebookskids.com
Library of Congress Cataloging-in-Publication Data is on file with the publisher.
Source of Production: Wing King Tong Paper Products Co. Ltd.,
Shenzhen, Guangdong Province, China
Date of Production: May 2021
Run Number: 5021664
Printed and bound in China.
WKT 10 9 8 7 6 5 4 3 2 1

When Beaver wandered into the valley, he heard
the most exciting sound in the entire world…

Running water!

The sound made Beaver's whole body quiver. It told him, "This is the place!"

A stream trickled through the valley.
Aspen, alder, and pine trees lined its banks.
Beaver got right to work.

An hour later…

Over the next few weeks,
Beaver cut down trees and
chewed off branches.

Squinting against the moonlight, he
wove the branches across the stream.
Soon, a pond began to form.

In the new pond, Beaver fashioned himself a safe, cozy lodge.

It wasn't long before a
female beaver arrived.

It was a match made
in beaver heaven.

Beaver's new pond attracted other animals that hadn't been there before.

The pond's rising water killed nearby trees, and beetles arrived to munch on the dead wood.

Woodpeckers soon followed to enjoy a beetle grub banquet!

PECK
PECK PECK PECK
PECK

Over time, the pond created a rich community of plants and animals. For Beaver, life seemed good.

Until one day…

Otter showed up.

Otter couldn't have been more
different from Beaver. He ate fish,
frogs, and crayfish—not plants
and bark. He powered himself
through the water with his tail.

Otter fished in Beaver's pond and found safety there,
but never helped make the dam stronger.

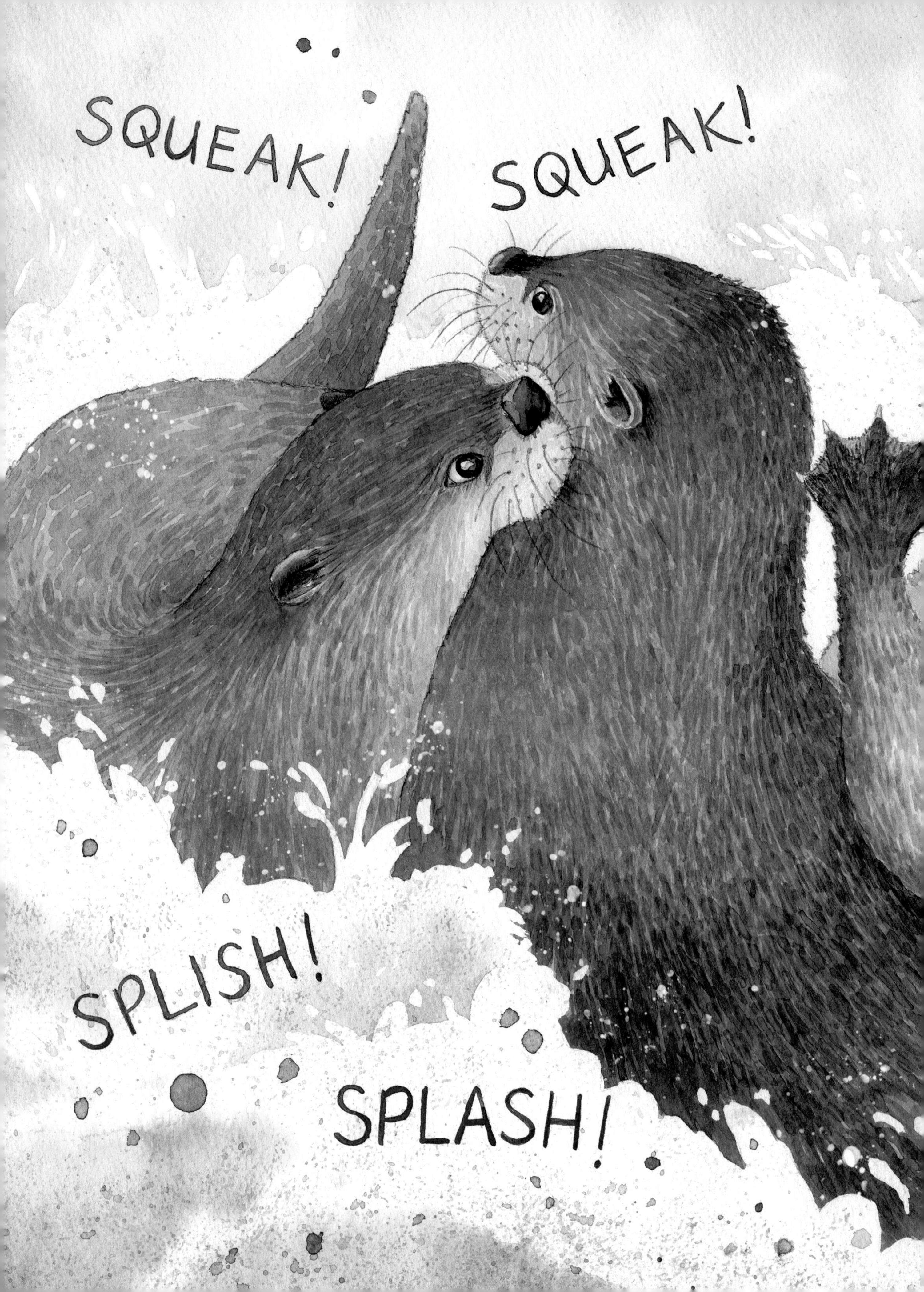
SQUEAK!
SQUEAK!
SPLISH!
SPLASH!

To make matters worse, more otters
arrived—a mom with her pups.
They also fished the pond and
wrestled and splashed and chattered.

What a racket!

whoosh

Come winter, the pond froze over and life quieted
down—all except for the otters.
While Beaver and his mate rested, the otters
turned the top of Beaver's lodge into a playground!
They scampered all over it and slid down the sides
as if it were a toboggan run.

And then things got worse.

One cold day, Beaver made a shocking discovery.
The pond level had dropped!
He heard trickling water and hurried to the dam.
There, he found a gaping hole.

Guess who made it?

The otters.

Beaver and his mate
quickly repaired the dam,
but the otters did the
same thing again.

And again!

GRUMBLE
GRUMBLE
GRUM
B
L
E

Beaver grunted—and
kept fixing the dam.

When spring sunlight melted the pond, however, Beaver had other things to think about besides otters.

Inside the lodge, Beaver's mate gave birth to three mewing beaver babies. While she nursed the new kits, Beaver brought her fresh bark to eat.

Meanwhile, Mama otter had new babies of her own. She raised the otter pups in a den at the edge of the pond.

This didn't keep the otters from coming around Beaver's lodge. Every once in a while, Beaver hissed loudly and charged at the otters. As usual, the otters didn't stay away for long.

HISSS

Eventually, though, Beaver and the otters grew used to each other.

Beaver and his mate built new dams along the stream and created new ponds. They dug canals to help them reach new trees for eating and building.

The otters swam through these ponds and canals. They caught fish and crayfish in them too.

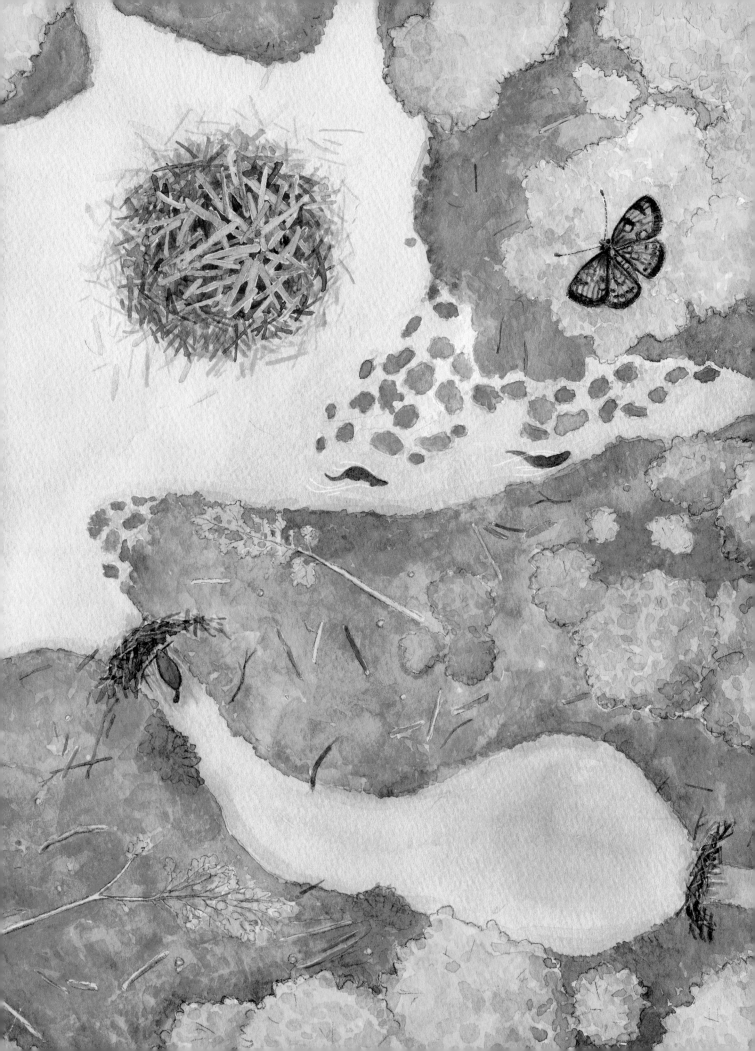

Over time, the valley transformed into a healthier, more interesting habitat for many different plants and animals.

The otters were not Beaver's favorite neighbors, but they weren't trying to be a nuisance. They just had different ways of doing things.

Beaver and Otter would never become best friends,
but that doesn't really matter. In their new home,
they sort of get along.

And that is enough.

AMAZING ADAPTATIONS

Beavers and river otters are perfectly suited for the water. Beaver young, called kits, can swim and walk within a few minutes of being born. Adult beavers can stay underwater for fifteen minutes. River otters move their body and tail up and down to speed through the water. They're not only expert swimmers—they're also underwater acrobats.

BEAVER

Herbivore (plant eater): eats the green layer under the bark of trees and also aquatic plants.

Flat tail for steering while swimming. Slapping it on water sends a warning. Used for balance when sitting.

Webbed back feet for swimming.

Claws on front paws for digging and carrying.

Ears and nostrils close to keep out water.

Clear eyelids act like goggles for seeing underwater.

Large front teeth contain iron that makes them strong, and also orange.

Beaver teeth never stop growing, but gnawing on wood keeps them from getting too long.

RIVER OTTER

Flexible body shaped like a torpedo for twisting and turning underwater.

Carnivore (meat eater): eats fish, crayfish, frogs, etc.

Long, strong tail for swimming and steering in water and for balancing when standing.

Webbed feet with claws for swimming and holding onto slippery prey.

Clear eyelids act like goggles for seeing underwater.

Ears and nostrils close to keep out water.

Sharp teeth for catching, grinding, and crushing prey—mostly fish.

Long sensitive whiskers help find prey in dark and cloudy water.

NATURE'S ARCHITECTS AND ENGINEERS

Beavers stay safe from coyotes, wolves, mountain lions, and other predators by building a home surrounded by water. Their lodge might look like just a pile of sticks, but it keeps beavers warm and dry through cold winters.

Before beavers can build their lodge, they usually need to build a dam across a stream and make a deep pond. The world's largest beaver dam is 2800 feet (850 m.) long. That's a lot of engineering for a four-foot (1.2 m.) rodent! Not all beavers live in lodges, though. Some dig burrows in the bank of a river or stream.

By making a home for themselves, beavers create a healthy habitat for hundreds of species of plants and animals, increasing a place's biodiversity. Because beavers are responsible for supporting an entire ecosystem, they are called a **keystone species**.

Otter Showed Up

Beaver ponds are favorite homes for otters. Ponds have more fish and other food than fast-running streams or rivers. The pond's banks are safe places for otters to make their dens and raise pups.

Otters must have very clean water to survive. If you see otters in a habitat, it usually means the **ecosystem** is healthy. That's why river otters are called an **indicator species**.

Sort of Get Along

Beavers and otters have a special kind of relationship. By creating ponds, beavers help otters. As far as we know, otters do not help beavers, but they usually don't hurt them either. Scientists call this a **commensal relationship**.

Sometimes otters can be a real nuisance for beavers, especially when they break open a dam in winter. Otters probably do this to let them reach the next pond without risking coming out onto land where predators can spot them. A break in a dam also lowers the water level under the ice. This makes it easier to catch fish and gives otters an air pocket to breathe in. Beavers are wary of having otters near their kits. When beavers are bothered by otters, they often hiss, charge, and shoo them away.

LITERACY CONNECTION

Read-Aloud Tips

Show the book cover and read the title and names of the author and illustrator.

1. Ask: What do you know about beavers and otters? Depending on the children's answers, you may need to point out that a river otter is different from a sea otter. A sea otter lives in salt water (oceans). A river otter lives in fresh water (rivers, lakes, and ponds). A river otter that lives near the coast may go into the ocean to hunt for food, but it lives in fresh water.

2. Ask: What do the words "Sort of" in the title tell you about the relationship of Beaver and Otter?

3. While reading, give special emphasis and expression to the words in large letters that make a sound: CRASH, MEW, PECK, SQUEAK, SPLASH, WHOOSH, GRUMBLE, HISS.

4. After reading, ask: How do Beaver and Otter sort of get along? What does the last sentence mean: "And that is enough"? Is there someone you would like to get along with better? What might you do to make that happen?

5. Conclude by looking at the cover again. Read the subtitle and discuss the meanings of "grit" and "patience."

Social Emotional Learning

Learning about the relationship between the beavers and otters is a natural springboard to teaching about relationship skills, one of the core competencies in social and emotional learning. It includes the ability to communicate clearly, listen well, cooperate with others, resist inappropriate social pressure, negotiate conflict constructively, and seek and offer help when needed.

Explain to children that problems and conflicts will happen even between the best of friends, but they have choices about how to handle the situation. The first thing they can do is to stop and take a breath. This will help them feel calm. Then they can make a choice about what to do next:

- Walk away and let it go.
- Tell the person to STOP.
- Go to another activity.
- Use an "I" message to express feelings.
- Apologize.
- Talk it out.
- Find a compromise.

- Ignore it.
- Wait and cool off.

SCIENCE CONNECTION

Commensal Relationships

A commensal relationship like the one in this story isn't one you hear much about, yet this kind of relationship abounds in nature. River otters aren't the only animals that benefit from beaver dams. Fish, herons, moose, turtles, and many other species "get along" with beavers. Other examples of commensal relationships include: bluebirds building nests inside holes drilled by woodpeckers, and barnacles attaching to whales to be carried to new locations for food. Ask children to notice commensal relationships in their neighborhood.

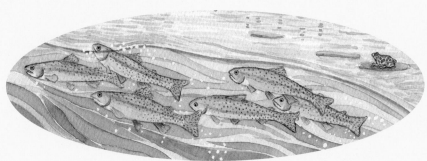

STEAM Activities

Beavers are second only to humans in their ability to manipulate and change their environment.

For interactive STEAM lessons kids can use at home or school, the following are available to download at https://www.sourcebooks.com/library.html

- **Build like a Beaver** – Work with others to build a beaver dam using craft supplies.

- **Compare and Contrast** – Create a Venn diagram to show how beavers and otters are the same and different.

- **Community of Critters** – Take a closer look at the illustrations in the book to find different animals and plants that live in and around the beaver pond.

Sneed B. Collard III is the author of more than eighty-five beloved books for young people. In 2006, Sneed was awarded the prestigious Washington Post-Children's Book Guild Award for Nonfiction for his body of work. He makes his home in Missoula, Montana where he often gets to observe beavers and otters. Learn more about Sneed at his website sneedbcollardiii.com and follow the birding adventures of Sneed and his son at fathersonbirding.com. Also check out his YouTube channel for his latest videos about birds and books.

Meg Sodano grew up in Connecticut, exploring the woodlands and seashore, and drawing her favorite animals. She studied natural science illustration at Rhode Island School of Design and animal science at the University of Vermont. She has visited many places where beavers live, trekking across dams and listening to kits mewing inside lodges. She still marvels at the beavers' engineering talents and their ability to create wetland habitats that benefit a whole array of wildlife. Meg's own lodge is located in Albany, NY.

May We Also Recommend These Nature Awareness Books

Scampers Thinks Like a Scientist—Scampers is no ordinary mouse—she knows how to investigate. Her infectiously experimental spirit will have young readers eager to think like scientists, too!

There's a Bug on My Book—All sorts of critters hop, fly, wiggle, and slide across the pages of this book, engaging children's imaginations while introducing them to the animals in the grass beneath their feet.

Pass the Energy, Please!—Everyone is somebody's lunch. In this upbeat rhyming story, the food chain connects herbivores, carnivores, insects, and plants together in a fascinating circle of players.

Wonderful Nature, Wonderful You—Nature can be a great teacher. With a light touch especially suited to children, this twentieth anniversary edition evokes feelings of calm acceptance, joy, and wonder. A delight for all ages.